Markie

and the Hammond Cousins

Wanda M. Yoder

Christian Light Publications, Inc.
Harrisonburg, Virginia 22802

MARKIE AND THE HAMMOND COUSINS

Christian Light Publications, Inc., Harrisonburg, Virginia 22802
©1994 by Christian Light Publications, Inc.
Printed in the United States of America

4th printing, 2007

Cover and Inside art: Ruth Yoder
Cover Design: Jotham Yoder

ISBN 978-0-87813-556-1

Dedicated to

all Down syndrome children
everywhere,

but especially to

Russell, Andrea,
and Andrew,

our three very special cousins.

Other titles in
the **Hammond Cousins Series**
by Wanda Yoder

Ricky and the Hammond Cousins

The Hammond cousins are first bewildered, then exasperated, and finally compassionate as they learn to relate to a boy with a hyperactive disorder.

In Memory of Michael

The excited Hammond sisters could hardly wait for the birth of the new baby. When Michael died, they were crushed. This tender story offers insights to finding comfort in the face of disappointment and grief.

Contents

1

Markie—
A Very Special Cousin

Barry's words came out rather garbled and breathy. He was hanging upside down from the crossbar at the end of Grandpa Hammond's rusty old swing set. Just then his cousin Jeff gave him a punch in the stomach and Barry came down gracefully without hurting himself a bit, although his freckled face was so red you could hardly see the spots.

"What I was trying to say," he began again, "is that our family get-togethers are never going to be the same now that Uncle Loren and Aunt Bess are moving here to live closer to Grandpas. And Markie, of course."

"And Markie, of course," Jeff repeated with a bit of scorn. "That's where the difference is

1

going to come in. We'll have him tagging along after us all the time."

"What's so wrong with Markie?" Marilyn asked, her nine-year-old sunburned face sweet and innocent.

"I suppose you've been too dumb to notice that he's retarded," Jeff said bluntly.

"Of course, I know he's mentally handicapped," Marilyn retorted, flipping her auburn braids back over her shoulders. "He's a Down syndrome child. I've known that for a long time, but what's so awful about that?"

"If you were a little smarter yourself, maybe you would get the implications," Jeff said loftily. "A mongoloid never matures beyond a certain level. I doubt that Markie will ever know much more than he does now."

Jeff's brother Steve was lying prone on the grass, his hands resting on his plump stomach that held one too many pieces of Grandma Hammond's good old-fashioned shoofly pie. Now he sat up and looked reproachfully at Jeff. "You are not to say 'mongoloid.' Mother said so. He has Down syndrome. That's something to do with his genes. He has the wrong amount or something like that. But—" he added honestly, "I guess I'm not so happy about them moving

2

here either. *Now*, we see him once or twice a year, but when they move here, it will be about every time we come to Grandpa's."

"And he gets mad so easily," Barry said, his hazel eyes twinkling mischievously. "Remember that time I snitched his pie when we were eating outside, and I told him that probably the dog got it? Old Lassie got the worst scolding you ever heard."

"Meanie!" Marilyn said.

"Oh, I told him later that I took it, but I don't think he understood. He kept saying, 'Dumb dog! Dumb dog!'"

Silence settled over the group of Hammond cousins as they sat remembering. In the stillness they could hear the bumblebees as they hovered over the roses or bumbled among the phlox.

Jeff, at twelve, was long and lank, and too much sock showed between the bottoms of his blue jeans and his size 7 sneakers. He and Steve, who was ten, were the sons of Tim Hammond, and like many of the Hammonds, they had black hair and snappy dark eyes. Jeff had very little patience with his chubby younger brother; indeed, he had little patience with anyone who could not keep up with his

3

line of thought or action.

Steve did not move unnecessarily, but although he often rested his round little body, his brain was active, and it was often his remarks that brought merriment to their little group.

Barry was eleven and full of tricks, to the despair of his parents and his long-suffering teachers. His last name was not Hammond but Martin, because it was his mother who belonged to the Hammond family.

Markie was also eleven, and a Zook. His mother, Bess, was the eldest in the Hammond family, and Markie was their youngest child who had come trailing behind several other brothers and sisters.

Marilyn's father was Alex Hammond, but she did not look the least bit like her Hammond cousins. There was a sweetness about her that few of the other cousins possessed.

Of course, there were other Hammond grandchildren at this family get-together. There were several smaller children playing house on the front steps of the vine-covered porch. Several big brothers were shooting baskets from the cement pad in front of the garage. Jeff, Barry, and Steve had asked to play too, but they had been told there wasn't room for more.

The older girls were giggling on a blanket out under the lilac bushes. One of the girls detached herself from the group and came toward the younger children. She looked a little sad as she plopped down beside Steve on the grass. She tried to arrange her skirts gracefully over her legs like the big girls did, but somehow the effect was not the same. At thirteen it is not always easy for a girl to be graceful.

"What's the matter, Sue?" Barry asked. "Did the conversation over there get syrupy? All about boys and such stuff?"

Sue shrugged. "What were you talking about?" she returned.

"About Markie coming," Jeff said. "We're not so enthusiastic about his coming into this community and being at all our gatherings."

"I don't know what you have to worry about," Sue said. "At least he won't be living really close to you, and he won't be coming to your church. Pity Barry, Marilyn, and me. We live here, and we'll have to claim him as our cousin."

"Don't pity me," Marilyn said promptly. "I

5

don't see what is so bad about having Markie around. He's been playing with us ever since we were small."

"Not on a regular basis though," Jeff said. "You can stand anything once or twice a year, but I guess you'll get mighty tired of having a mongoloid around soon enough."

"Down syndrome," Steve said automatically. "It sounds more respectful."

"Down syndrome, then. Maybe, Marilyn, you can just entertain Markie when we are having Hammond gatherings. You are really too young to be with us anyway."

"I can do anything you can do," Marilyn flashed, her dark eyes sparkling. "Want to race?"

"Not now," Jeff answered, remembering the last time she had challenged him. That time he had become tangled up with his long legs and she had scampered past him to the applause of all the aunts and uncles. Jeff did not like to admit that he was a loser in any game, but he had to admire plucky little Marilyn. That was why she was included with the middle cousins instead of being relegated to the younger set.

"I have to wonder why God permits mentally handicapped people to be born," Sue said quietly.

6

"Why didn't He make Markie perfect like the rest of us?"

"Perfect!" Barry hooted. "So you think you're perfect. Then why do you have to wear braces on your teeth, and why do you have pimples?"

Sue blushed miserably. "I-I mean we have good minds and sound bodies and . . ."

"Mother said handicapped people help us to be kind," Marilyn said. "At least that's the way we *ought* to act," she added, frowning at Jeff, Barry, and Steve.

"You have to admit, though," Jeff insisted, "that having Markie around is going to be a problem. Can you imagine him sitting here with us having a serious conversation? Why, much of the time he can't even talk clearly enough for us to understand him."

"I can understand him," Steve said. "It's a little like listening to a toddler. If you want to understand badly enough, you usually can. Maybe if we pretend he is our little brother, we will think he is cute, and we will try harder to understand what he says. He does say cute things sometimes."

"He was cute when he was scolding Old Lassie," Barry grinned.

"That wasn't very nice," Sue said. "Mother

said that is why they are moving into this community. Where they live now, people make so much fun of Markie that he is getting sassy, and sometimes he gets so mad he just trembles. Uncle Loren and Aunt Bess want him to grow up sweet and good even if he is mentally handicapped. But it isn't going to be easy having him around. There aren't any other children like him at church. I don't know why he has to be a Hammond."

"He's not a Hammond; he's a Zook," Steve said. "But I suppose everyone will know you're related."

"Maybe if we make it clear we don't appreciate his company he'll stick with the little children," Jeff said hopefully. "But I doubt it will work. He knows he's our age and he always hangs around us. In some ways he's not so dumb."

Sue sighed. "If he just looked more normal. But he doesn't even look like other people. His face is so flat and his eyes so small, and his arms look so long for as short as he is. And sometimes he slobbers. . . ."

"If only he were perfect like you," Barry snickered.

Sue blushed again and looked away. Barry

could be so hateful sometimes. She felt like reminding him of his freckles.

"It takes all kinds of people to make a world," Steve quoted sagely from his prone position on the grass. It sounded so silly that they were all smiling when Uncle Jerry walked up.

"It looks as though you children are enjoying yourselves," he said, sitting down beside Sue. "Mind if I join you? The old folks are talking farming, the young fellows playing ball make me tired just watching them sweat, and those girls are probably talking about dress material which I know nothing about, so . . . well, what were you young-uns doing with yourselves today?"

The children liked Uncle Jerry even though they could never quite figure him out. He looked old and young at the same time. His body was trim and strong, but there was a tiredness about him, even though he worked hard and did not seem to notice it. There was a sadness in his eyes as soon as he stopped smiling. A jagged scar ran down the side of his face and disappeared into his shirt collar making him look almost wicked. Yet there did not seem to be any wickedness in this gentle uncle who lived all alone in a trailer a mile or so from

Grandpa Hammond's. Sue and Jeff could faintly remember many years ago when the family seemed to do a lot of praying for Uncle Jerry. Later there had been a motorcycle accident and much more praying. Now Uncle Jerry's name was still often mentioned in prayer but the children did not really know why. The Uncle Jerry they knew was good and kind and patient and upright.

Marilyn moved over and sat next to Uncle Jerry. "It's Markie," she said earnestly. "The others think it is going to be just awful having him here all the time. Do you think it will be such a problem for us?"

Uncle Jerry smiled down at the little girl. "It will be a problem if you children make it a problem," he said.

"I think *he* will be a problem no matter what *we* do," Jeff contradicted darkly. "Retards just don't fit in with other people without causing trouble."

"That's not the nicest term to use in reference to those who are mentally handicapped," Uncle Jerry reproved with a disappointed look on his face.

"Takes too long to say Down syndrome," Jeff objected. "And anyway, there are all kinds of things that make people retarded. There's a girl who goes to our church and school and they don't know why she is a retard—oops—is retarded. But she sure is a problem. She takes so much of the teacher's time. And she never plays very well in any of our games. Most of the time she plays with the little children."

Uncle Jerry nodded and continued, "I prefer calling retarded people the mentally handicapped. It sounds nicer and explains the problem the individual has. And it would be well if we would remember that *all* of us are handicapped in some way or another."

"Not Sue. She's perfect. She said so." Barry grinned provokingly.

Sue did not bother to reply. Somehow with Uncle Jerry near she did not feel the need to defend herself. He always made her feel worthwhile just by being herself. Indeed, his acceptance of them as children was the reason he was always welcomed into their circle.

For the first time Steve sat up from his sprawled position on the grass. "What do you mean we are handicapped?" he demanded. "Being handicapped means there is something wrong with your body, or like Markie, that you can't think right. There is nothing wrong with

11

any of us."

"Except Sue has pim—" but a look from Uncle Jerry silenced Barry.

"Perhaps it means something else too," Jeff said, interest aflame in his dark eyes. He loved enlarging his vocabulary and used all the big words for which he could find occasion and then some.

"I think it does," Uncle Jerry said. "Run in and get Grandma's big dictionary. Tell her Uncle Jerry wants it or she won't let you bring it outside."

Jeff was soon back, carrying the fat gray dictionary. "Read all the meanings and see if you can find any that may relate to you children," Uncle Jerry ordered him.

Jeff read silently while the other children fidgeted on the grass. At last Jeff shoved the book at Uncle Jerry with a puzzled look. "I'm not quite sure what you mean," he said.

"What about the second meaning?" Uncle Jerry asked. "It reads, 'a disadvantage that makes achievement unusually difficult.' I'm thinking about your bad habits. As long as you have them, you will have a difficult time achieving all that you could otherwise. They are a handicap to your character development.

The fortunate fact about bad habits is that if you are aware of them, you can work to eliminate them altogether. It is true that Markie can never overcome all his handicap, but if you normal children overcome yours, you may well overlook some of his."

Jeff tossed his black hair out of his eyes and said, "I don't think I have any bad habits that make achievement unusually difficult."

"And *that* is your bad habit, or rather, poor character quality, that is going to make it hard for you to be all that you ought to be," Uncle Jerry said. Seeing Jeff's confusion, he went on to explain. "You are overly confident of your abilities and your worth. You have a tendency to run over other people. You like to be the best in whatever you do and it is hard for you to appreciate other children when they get ahead of you in something. I've seen you get so upset while playing games that you hollered at the others, threw things, or stomped off."

"Oh!" Jeff said, looking suddenly as wilted as the daisy he was pulling apart in his hands.

"Don't be so downhearted," Uncle Jerry smiled. "Being an achiever is good, but you need to rejoice when others do well and have more patience with those who are slow."

"What about me?" Sue asked with a troubled air.

"Your handicap? Well, it's *not* your teeth or your complexion," Uncle Jerry said emphatically. "You would do well to be less concerned with your outside, and be thinking more of your inside. God loves you as He made you, but I'm sure He would like to see you happier, kinder, and more concerned about others than yourself. You don't need to be embarrassed because of the goofs you make unless they are things that are actually wrong. Then you *should* be ashamed and make things right."

"I know what you are going to say about me," Steve said mournfully, patting his stomach. "You are going to tell me I shouldn't eat so much."

"And work more," Uncle Jerry agreed. "I've noticed you will go to great ends to avoid work, and if your dad merely mentions a job, your face turns upside down. That is a real handicap to your development, you know."

Steve sighed and sat up straight, trying to look ambitious. He looked so comical that the others had to laugh.

"What do you think your character handicap might be?" Uncle Jerry asked Barry, who was beginning to look very uncomfortable.

"Everyone says I'm a pest," Barry muttered.

"Well, are you?" Uncle Jerry asked.

"I'm just having fun," Barry defended himself.

"At another's expense, I've noticed," Uncle Jerry said drily. "Humor makes for a happier world, but not when it hurts other people. You simply need to work at being kinder."

"I know," Barry admitted, glancing over at Sue with a look that said better than words that he was sorry he had given her such a rough time about her appearance.

"What about me?" Marilyn whispered.

Uncle Jerry looked gently at the little girl whose pixie face always gazed so adoringly at his. "Do you always say the truth and nothing but the truth, Marilyn?" he asked.

Her face clouded. "I—I think so."

"You mean it was true what you were telling Barry earlier today, that you had to shell a thousand pails of peas? Do your neighbors really have a million chickens? Did you really tell your baby sister a hundred times to stay out of your doll dishes?"

"No-o," Marilyn said. "I was just 'zaggerating, I guess."

"Well, that's a bad habit that is going to get you into trouble," Uncle Jerry said. "Think before you talk and say only the truth."

Uncle Jerry smiled at the sober bunch of children before him. "I do think," he said, "that if you concern yourselves with your own handicaps and work at overcoming them, then Markie won't be much of a problem for you. You may even learn to enjoy having him for a very special cousin."

Just then a call for ice-cream treats drifted across the lawn. The children jumped to their feet and raced for the house. All except Steve. With self-control, he measured his steps with Uncle Jerry's, and he was the last one to get his ice-cream cone.

2

Barry Martin— Pest or Partner?

Barry Martin stared at his father in dismay. "But, Dad," he almost wailed, "you don't mean to say that Markie is going to be in our Sunday school class? Not the juniors! He can't read nearly well enough to be in our class. Why can't he be in the primaries or even with the preschoolers? He'll never fit into *our* class."

Lester Martin did not look the least bit disturbed by his son's outburst. "It's all been decided," he said firmly. "I've talked it over with Loren and Bess and your teacher, and they all agree that Markie can be happy with his own age group, at least for a time. Perhaps later, circumstances will change, but right now the other classrooms are plenty full. So he will be in yours."

Barry knew his father was the Sunday school superintendent and that if he said it was settled, it was; yet he somehow had to convince his father that Markie ought not to be in his class. "But, Dad," he said, "Markie always sat with Uncle Loren during Sunday school when they visited here. Because Markie is retarded, don't you think that is the best way?"

"No, I don't," Dad said. "Markie needs to be accepted in every way possible, and there is no reason he can't sit in Sunday school with you. He loves stories, and even if he doesn't understand *everything*, he will understand *some* things. Best of all he will feel loved and accepted by the rest of you children."

Barry sighed. "Well, I don't think he will feel loved and accepted. The other children will probably think he is a nuisance and make fun of him when the teacher isn't looking."

Dad suddenly became very stern. "Listen here, Barry," he said. "There is to be none of that! I hope you realize that the way you treat your cousin will pretty much set the course for the way the other children treat him. If you respect him just as much as if he were your best friend, then they will too. He won't be a problem if you don't make him one."

Barry stuttered in amazement. "W-why, that's just what Uncle Jerry said!"

Dad smiled. "And it's true. Why don't you take that as a personal challenge? Determine that Markie is your friend, that he is not a problem, and that if he does hit some rough spots, you will help him over them. How about it, Son?"

Barry knew Dad would take nothing but "yes" for an answer, but he did not want to say the word that would make him duty-bound to help Markie all he could.

"Well, Son?" Dad said again, and Barry raised reluctant eyes to his. "All right," he promised. "I'll try."

The next Sunday morning it was cold and rainy. As Barry picked up his Bible and Sunday school quarterly to leave for church with the family, he could not help but hope that perhaps Markie would not be able to attend. He often had colds and stayed at home with Aunt Bess. It would only put off the evil day if Markie was not in Sunday school, but it would give Barry time to explain to the other boys what Markie was like so it would not be such a shock. Somehow Barry had never told his friends that he had a retarded cousin, or that he would be attending their church. He had always pretended that Markie was no relative of his whenever they had come to visit.

But Markie was there. In the men's coatroom

he trotted up to Barry with shining eyes, and showed him his Bible, Sunday school book, and pen. "I will go with you!" he announced with a broad smile.

For a moment his pleasure was contagious, and Barry smiled back.

In Sunday school Markie sat quietly while the teacher went over the lesson. Brother Tom thoughtfully did not have the children read verses as usual, but read the Scripture himself. He explained things thoroughly, and Markie seemed to understand. Markie had a good memory, and soon he could say the first part of the memory verse himself. He formed syllables that sounded almost like the correct words for the parts he did not know. But when it came time to check the work they were supposed to do at home, Markie was dismayed to see that he was the only one who had not written anything in his book. Tears came into his eyes. "Not done! Not done!" he blubbered.

Barry was embarrassed. He did not like to see anyone cry, least of all a boy his own age, and in Sunday school of all places.

But Brother Tom did not seem upset. "That's all right, Markie," he consoled him. "You just listen while the others read what they have written. If you think they have an answer wrong, just raise your hand and tell us. All right, John, what is the answer to the first question?"

Markie sat quietly, but every now and then Barry could hear him mutter, "Not done! Not done!"

It was later while the preacher was speaking on Christian compassion that a noble thought came to Barry. Brother David had just quoted the words of Jesus, "Inasmuch as ye have done it unto one of the least of these my brethren, ye have done it unto me." He explained that Jesus meant that doing kind deeds for others was like doing them for Him.

Barry thought of a kind deed that would make Markie enjoy Sunday school more, but he did not want to do it. Surely it was Aunt Bess's responsibility, or perhaps Brother Tom should do it. Markie would probably not cooperate anyway. It was not worth the bother. All kinds of excuses came to Barry's mind, and he did not hear much of the rest of the sermon. After church his family had dinner with another family from church, and Barry pushed all thoughts of Markie from his mind.

But Markie and the kind deed Barry ought

to do for him kept coming into Barry's thoughts all through the week, and finally on Saturday afternoon he went to his mother and told her all about it.

"Why, that's a wonderful idea," she beamed. "Why don't you just call Aunt Bess and see what she says about it."

Immediately after supper Barry got on his bicycle and rode the two miles to Markie's house. Aunt Bess met him at the door with a big smile. "You are a dear boy to even think of coming," she said, giving Barry a kiss before he could dodge. Markie thrived on hugs and kisses, but Barry avoided them if at all possible. "I know I should have helped him myself," she went on, "but time has a way of getting away, and I don't get everything done that I should. And it will take a lot of time. I hope you have plenty of patience."

Barry did not know whether he would have enough patience or not, but he had started on this venture and he would go through with it. That was one thing about Barry; whether the task at hand was mischief or work, he carried it through to the end. The mischief had gotten him into more trouble than he cared to think about. But this was work, and he had better get on with it.

Just then Markie bounded into the room, his face flooded with joy. He was waving his Bible, Sunday school quarterly, and pencil around, and prancing and dancing. "Do my work, now," he shouted. "Brother Tom will be glad, glad, glad!"

Aunt Bess got them situated at the dining room table and then left them to their studies. Barry soon saw that although Markie could read a little, it would take him too long to read through all the material himself. The story was about the stoning of Stephen as recorded in Acts. Because Markie did not seem to understand the lesson text, Barry asked Aunt Bess for the Bible story book and read it from there and showed him the picture of wicked men picking up stones to throw at Stephen. That seemed to help Markie understand what the lesson was about.

Markie laboriously wrote all the words in the blanks as Barry spelled them out to him. It took a long time and prickles of irritation raced up and down Barry's spine. At last they were done and Markie jubilantly laid down his pencil. He put his face very close to Barry's and said emphatically, "You good boy, Barry. Good like Stephen. I love you!"

Although Barry felt more tired than he had in a long time, he could not deny the warm feeling that encircled his heart. The next day when Markie announced to Brother Tom that Barry had helped him with his work and he saw Brother Tom's approval, Barry felt well rewarded. He resolved to help Markie every week. Teasing Markie had always been fun, but helping him made Barry feel better inside.

A week or two later, Aunt Bess and Markie came for a visit one sunny afternoon. While the women were taking a tour of the garden and fussing over the flowers, Barry led Markie out to the chicken yard.

"Look here, Markie," Barry said. "See all these different kinds of chickens? Now just watch. When I call, two of them will come running. They are my pets. Here C-C-C-Cock! Here K-K-K-Katie!"

Two chickens, a hen and a rooster, came scuttling around the corner of the chicken house and up to Barry. They eyed Markie warily, but skipped around at Barry's feet as if they were expecting something. He stooped down with his hands outstretched, palms up. In his hands he had several kernels of corn. The chickens ate the corn and then hopped onto his hands. Slowly Barry stood up, the two chickens still standing on his hands.

"Er-er-er-er!" Barry crowed. Immediately the little rooster hopped up onto his shoulder and then onto his head. There he flapped his wings and crowed for all he was worth as if to out-crow his master.

"Down, Cock," Barry demanded, and the rooster hopped back down onto his hand. Then Barry made the clucky sound of a hen and the little hen hopped up onto his head. "I can't make her cluck on purpose," Barry said, "but isn't she cute?"

"Do it again," Markie shouted. "Do it again!" He was so excited that he was jumping all over, and Barry had to tell him to stand still so the chickens would not run away. Barry had the chickens do their stunt over and over again until he ran out of corn.

"Mama see," Markie begged, so Barry oblig-ingly got more corn and carried the little hen and rooster up to the house. It would be fun to show off his pets to another appreciative audi-ence, for since he was helping Markie with his Sunday school work, Aunt Bess seemed to think Barry was just wonderful.

Barry was the middle child in his family, and sometimes he thought all they appreciated him for was as a runner of errands or someone to blame for any mischief that happened around the place. Of course, usually he *was* the cause of the mischief, but he wished they would notice when he did things right too. It seemed to him they never did. It would be nice to have someone admire him, even if it were just his aunt and retarded cousin.

Just as they got to the house, someone cried out, "Oh, look there! There's a hot-air balloon over the woods!" and everyone raced behind the house to watch it. Barry thrust the two chickens through the door into the screened porch so they would not get away, grabbed Markie's hand, and raced after the others. The whole family, Aunt Bess, and Markie watched the balloon elevate and dip until it drifted away and they could not see it anymore. Then they went back to the house.

Barry remembered his chickens at the same time he met Mother at the door looking very upset. "Barry," she said, "this *has* to be one of your tricks again! Come in here and see the mess those chickens of yours have made of this porch!"

Barry tried to explain what had happened, but Mother was unimpressed. "You could have let them go, you know," she said disgustedly. "Aunt Bess and I are planning to run over to Uncle Jerry's to take him this cake and do some cleaning. I was going to take you along to be company for Markie and maybe to visit Uncle Jerry if he's there, but it looks as though you have cleaning to do right here. Re-pot that fern carefully, and it looks as if this violet needs some attention too. Sweep up that dirt entirely, and you'll probably need to mop. When will you ever learn to think before you act?"

Feeling misunderstood by Mother and betrayed by his pets, Barry looked in dismay at the porch. Cock must have hopped up onto the hanging fern and got it swinging until it crashed to the floor. Some other plants had been trampled on or pecked at. Katie was back in the corner looking thoroughly miserable in her unusual environment. Barry caught the chickens and took them back out to the chicken yard, and then surveyed the mess again. First he needed to take care of the plants. Barry loved plants, and he was painstakingly picking up the pieces when a voice behind him asked, "What Markie do?"

"Markie!" Barry said with astonishment. "What are you doing here?"

"Going to clean up mess," Markie declared. "Dirty, dirty. Bad chickens. Bad Barry. Bad Markie."

"It's a mess all right," Barry agreed. "But I don't know what you can do about it."

"Clean up that," Markie said, pointing to the back of the couch where there was a pile of chicken manure.

Barry gulped. The couch was covered with a throw cover that could be washed, but Mother would certainly want him to take off all the manure that would come off. Markie disappeared into the house and came out with the dishrag. Barry was amused to think what Mother would say if Markie used that!

"Here are some paper towels," Barry suggested, hardly believing that Markie could really be of any use, or that he would volunteer to clean up chicken manure. Markie scrubbed diligently until he was done, however, and then helped sweep up the dirt.

Barry was still feeling blue about the whole mess when suddenly Markie patted him on the shoulder and said, "Be happy, Barry. Jesus loves you."

"How do you know?" Barry asked rather crossly.

Markie grinned. "'Cause. Listen!" He folded his small hands in front of him and began to sing, "Jesus loves me, this I know . . ." Barry listened in amazement as he sang the song perfectly in tune and with a sweetness that was a joy to hear. He sang three verses, and when he did not know the words he sang la-la-la and kept on.

"Do you know any more songs?" Barry asked. Singing was something he himself was not very good at, and he was astonished that Markie could sing so well.

Markie sang song after song of the sort little children love, and almost before Barry thought of the time, the porch was cleaned up and the mothers were back home.

All the next week the memory of Markie's singing rang in Barry's ears. He knew that singing was pure joy to Markie and that his retarded cousin would like it if they would sing in Sunday school. Brother Tom wasn't much of a singer, and they had never sung in class. What would happen if Barry suggested they sing for Markie's sake? Brother Tom would likely think it was a good idea, but what would the other boys think? Some of them thought singing was just for girls. None of the children had made fun of Markie yet, but what would they say if they were requested to sing "baby songs"?

At last Barry again went to Mother and asked her advice. She looked very pleased. "Why don't you call Brother Tom and hear what he says," she suggested. "For myself, I think it's a wonderful idea."

Barry gulped when Brother Tom thought it was a fine idea and suggested that Barry lead the songs. Barry promised to lead at least the first one.

Nervousness gripped him when he walked into class on Sunday with Markie proudly trotting beside him. He had to admit to himself that he enjoyed the feeling of making people happy, rather than being considered a pest, but this time he wondered if he had not gone too far. What would the boys think of him if he suggested they sing "Running Over," one of Markie's favorite songs?

After prayer, Brother Tom simply suggested that they sing. "Barry, why don't you lead the first one," he said.

Barry's throat felt tight, but he began to

sing, "Jesus Loves Me." Markie's face suddenly took on a glow and he began to sing too. He swung his legs and patted his knees in time to the music and looked as though he were thoroughly enjoying himself. The girls joined in enthusiastically, Marilyn's voice, sweet and clear, rising above the rest. Compelled by the atmosphere, the boys added their tones, and soon the musty little classroom rang with jubilant song. As soon as they finished one, Markie had another he wanted to sing, and to Barry's relief, he led the rest.

Once Barry glanced at Marilyn and saw her face turned to his in admiration. He was puzzled and then humbled to realize that this was her way of telling him she knew the singing was his doing and that she heartily approved.

Just then the door opened. It was Dad coming to take the roll and to pick up the offering envelope. He stood for a moment listening to them sing and then said, "That sounds wonderful, children. That is music to please the heart of God!" He looked for a long moment at Barry with a look that Barry could not remember seeing for quite a while, a look that said, "That nice boy is Barry Martin. I'm glad he is my son."

Flushed with happiness and contentment, Barry did not even squirm when Markie suddenly reached over and gave him a big hug. Then with an understanding smile, Brother Tom suggested they get on with their lesson.

3

Steve Hammond—
A Day at the Sale Barn

Steve Hammond managed to eat only three pancakes and two eggs this morning because of his many trips to the living room window to see if anyone had come in the lane.

"Why don't you just stay put once and get finished eating?" Mom said, looking at the clock. "You still have time left."

"I know," Steve said, "but I don't want to keep Uncle Jerry waiting. You know he has a load of steers, and he wants to get there early so we don't have to wait so long to unload. Feels like it could get hot today, too." He tried hard not to sound important, but going to the sale barn with Uncle Jerry was really special, and it was hard not to gloat over it, especially when Jeff sat there looking so envious. Of course, at times, they both had gone to the sale barn with Dad to sell little calves and cull cows, but going with Uncle Jerry to sell his steers was better yet.

"If Uncle Jerry comes with his truck and cattle trailer without you hearing him, he'll be gentleman enough to come to the door and let you know," Dad said with a chuckle.

"Besides that," Mother added, "you need to wash up. Be sure and get that dirty neck of yours clean. There is a shadow all around just above your collar."

"Oh, that's permanent dirt," Steve said quickly. "I can't get it off. I tried and tried last Saturday."

"Permanent dirt, indeed!" Mother sputtered. "There is no such thing. Come along to the bathroom and we'll see what we can do about that permanent dirt!"

Steve reluctantly went with Mother to the bathroom, and there she proceeded to soap down his chubby neck and scrub him thoroughly.

"I don't know why I have to be so clean," Steve grumbled. "I'm just going to the sale barn. Now if it were to the dentist . . ."

"You still wouldn't want to wash," Mother said. "There, that's better. Now Uncle Jerry won't need to be ashamed of you." She gave him a kiss before he could duck.

"Uncle Jerry's here," Jeff called, and with a merry good-bye, Steve was out the door.

"Good morning, Steve," Uncle Jerry said. "I see you still want to go along."

"Sure do!" Steve answered, and then stopped short, for sitting proudly on the front seat was Markie. Steve's heart sank. He had so much counted on being alone with Uncle Jerry, and now he had to share him with Markie, of all people. Not that Markie was so bad usually, but this was to be a special day. And what enjoyment could Markie get out of going to the sale barn?

Uncle Jerry must have seen the struggle and the resentment on Steve's face. He said brightly, "Markie has never been to a sale barn. I thought it would be a good experience for him, and then too, it's always so much fun to share a nice time with someone when everything is new to him."

Steve knew that was true, so he nodded and said, "Hi, Markie. Do you want to be in the middle or by the window?"

39

Markie chose the middle and soon they were on the way. It was forty miles to the sale barn, part of it on country roads and part of it on a four-lane state highway. Steve swallowed his disappointment in having Markie along and helped Uncle Jerry point out things of interest to Markie. They mentioned what was growing in each of the fields, and soon Markie could tell a hayfield from a cornfield. They counted horses and tractors and four-wheelers. They pointed out pigs and sheep and cows. Then they talked about the vehicles they were meeting. Markie became excited about the tractor-trailer trucks they saw. Without fail he would shout, "Semi! Semi!" as they zoomed past.

Steve tired of it and at last he said bluntly, "Markie, why don't you dry up? I'm tired of hearing you say, 'Semi, semi!' all the time."

Markie stuck out his lower lip, glared at Steve, and gave him a light punch in the stomach. "Dumb Steve!" he said.

Steve opened his mouth to give a similar retort, but a look from Uncle Jerry silenced him. He sighed and tried to shut his ears because no matter how much Uncle Jerry tried to divert his attention, Markie never missed a semi all the way to the sale barn.

40

At the sale barn there was only one load ahead of them, so they did not have long to wait. Steve admired how deftly Uncle Jerry backed the cattle trailer up to the unloading platform. He could do it just as well as Dad could, and that was very well.

Steve and Markie got out and watched from behind a metal gate as Uncle Jerry opened up the cattle trailer and started herding out the eight steers. A great big fat man was in the pen right behind the trailer slapping numbers onto the backs of each steer as it came out. He was the fattest man the boys had ever seen. Steve wondered where he ever found a place to buy such huge striped overalls. Even Markie noticed and muttered, "Fat man! Fat man!"

The steers knew Uncle Jerry and went out of the trailer obediently and on out another gate that a young fellow was opening and closing at the right time. But suddenly the last steer out seemed to go crazy and whirled around. He tried to get back into the trailer, but Uncle Jerry slammed the door shut just in time. The steer ran around and around the little pen and the fat man tried to chase him on out. Suddenly the steer charged the young fellow by the gate, who took one look at the confused animal and vaulted over the metal fence. The steer then shoved the fat man up against the metal bars and kept shoving him with his front shoulder. The big man's face got redder and redder and he hollered words Steve knew must be swear words. Uncle Jerry jumped into the pen and tried to get the steer to move, but it would not budge. The young fellow jumped back in, and this time he had a cattle prod. He poked it at the steer, and the electric current in the rod made the steer whirl away and go through the gate just as he was supposed to. Everyone breathed a sigh of relief, and the man massaged his middle where all the extra flesh would likely soon carry bruises.

"I'm sorry that happened," Uncle Jerry said. "I never knew there was a wild one in there or I would have warned you."

"You never can tell about animals," the man said, looking a little sheepish. "I should never have gone in there without a whip or a prod. There is such a thing as being too quick to beat an animal, but sometimes that is the only thing that saves your own hide."

"You may come back this way with me to the office," the young fellow said to Uncle Jerry.

"May I go up on the catwalk while you check

in the steers?" Steve asked Uncle Jerry.

The catwalk was an iron walkway that was suspended above the animal pens. When you were up there, you could see down over all the animals, and it was fun to watch them mill around in the pens below. You could see pens full of little calves, pens full of cows of all colors and breeds, and pens full of pigs of all sizes. Sometimes sheep filled the sale barn with the noise of their pathetic bleating. Once there was a horse sale, and they had bought their beautiful Morgan colt, Star.

"Sure, go on up," Uncle Jerry said. "Markie, do you want to go with him?"

Markie looked with fear at the stairs Steve was pointing to and vigorously shook his head. "Not going up there!" he said emphatically.

"Well, then you must come with me," Uncle Jerry said, taking Markie's hand and leading him through the gate that went into an alley between all the pens.

But suddenly Markie saw all the animals behind bars and he panicked. "I not go with you," he wailed. "Steer will get me!"

"No, it won't," Uncle Jerry said calmly. "They can't get here in the alley any more. See, I'm holding your hand." But Markie pulled back.

Tears poured down his cheeks and he began to blubber.

Steve heard the fuss and looked down from the catwalk. Uncle Jerry was looking uncomfortable as if he did not know what to do. He had to go back with the young fellow, but Markie was certainly being difficult. Usually he was obedient, but seeing the steer push the man must have unnerved him. The young fellow had a curious look on his face as if he were wondering how it would all come out.

Steve was disgusted. If Markie had not been along, he would have gone back with Uncle Jerry to check in the steers, and then they would have gone up on the catwalk and wandered around together. But now Markie was making an embarrassing fuss and spoiling everything. He was acting like a big baby. In fact, his behavior was just about what Steve would have expected of his little brother who had just turned three.

"Well, I guess you'll just have to sit in the truck then," Uncle Jerry said. "But I must come back in. You will have to be alone."

"No, no!" Markie wailed, and Uncle Jerry suddenly looked beaten.

Steve was thinking hard. He had told the

44

other cousins at the family reunion that understanding Markie was like understanding a toddler. If you wanted to understand badly enough, you could. He saw now that handling Markie was a great deal like caring for his little brother, and he had done that many times.

"Uncle Jerry, Uncle Jerry," he hollered down over the railing of the catwalk. "I'll come down and take care of Markie."

Uncle Jerry looked doubtful and relieved at the same time. "You can try," he said.

Steve galloped down off the catwalk and came to where Uncle Jerry and Markie stood. "Come, Markie," Steve said in a voice he hoped sounded both friendly and authoritative. "Let's go out to the truck. Maybe we can go see the little pigs on the way. Wouldn't you like to see the little pigs? They are *so* cute."

Markie stopped crying and wiped his eyes and blew his nose on the big white handkerchief he had in his pocket. He looked interested, so Steve led him over to where a man was unloading a bunch of feeder pigs. They were active, friendly little creatures, more curious than afraid. They only weighed about forty pounds each, so they were not big enough to look threatening to Markie. The owner seemed to take the situation into account and herded one little black-and-white pig up close to the fence and held it tightly so that Markie could reach through and touch it. It was a quick touch, but one that made Markie immensely delighted.

"Nice pig. Nice pig." Markie beamed.

They stood at a safe place on the unloading deck and watched another man unload a new-born calf. Steve chattered and explained things just as he would have done if Markie were his little brother, and he saw the tension slowly leave Markie. Markie was laughing and excited by the time Uncle Jerry returned.

Uncle Jerry looked very relieved. "Well, boys," he said. "I see you got along all right without me."

"I saw pigs and calves," Markie informed him brightly.

"You did? That's nice. Now let's go downtown for awhile. Then we'll come back and eat at the restaurant here. Then we'll watch the auction."

"Eat here?" Steve said, very surprised. "When I'm with Dad we always go to Hardee's or McDonald's. He says the food here is so expensive you have to sell an extra calf to pay for it."

Uncle Jerry smiled. "I know, but I want to treat some very special boys to a very special meal. Let's go."

First they went to a department store. Uncle Jerry was not in a hurry. "I don't go shopping very often," he explained. "And it isn't much fun to always go alone."

He looked at car waxes and batteries, headlights and mirrors, and he bought a mirror to replace one on the truck. He bought himself a pair of tennis shoes. "So I can play basketball with the boys," he explained. He bought a new white shirt. "I can't keep them white like a woman can," he said. He bought a new wastebasket to replace the one he had gotten too close to the incinerator and burned a hole in it.

Steve thought it seemed strange for a man to go up the aisles that had sheets, pillows, towels, and washcloths, but Uncle Jerry did and bought some dish towels and a bath towel set. "Uncle Jerry," he said, "you need a wife. Why don't you get married, anyway? Somewhere I am sure there is a woman who would make you a good wife."

Uncle Jerry got a strange look on his face. "Some things are hard to explain, my boy," he said gently. "But don't worry yourself over me.

I've got a very good family to help me along." He looked sad as he often did, but after awhile when he let the boys watch the fish, birds, and hamsters in the pet corner, and Markie got so excited he was jumping up and down, Uncle Jerry smiled again.

They went to a shoe store, and Uncle Jerry bought some work boots. He asked the boys' advice, and it was fun helping him decide whether he preferred brown or black.

Then they went to the grocery store and bought bread, cookies, and a few other things Uncle Jerry needed at home.

Steve was glad when they headed back to the sale barn, for he was getting very hungry. The restaurant was crowded, but they found a place where they could sit together, Uncle Jerry and Markie on one side of the table and Steve on the other. They looked at the menu and Steve became confused at the possibilities until Uncle Jerry suggested a roast beef plate. "After all," he said, "if I sell steers, we should do our part in eating beef, don't you think?" Markie nodded vigorously and Steve grinned. Being with Uncle Jerry was fun.

They were just starting to eat when the man who had gotten pushed by the steer came in and sat down. Steve watched out of the corner of his eye to see what the man would order. He ordered a roast beef plate with a big bowl of salad extra on which he poured a tremendous amount of salad dressing. He drank coffee and put lots of sugar and cream in it. *Now* Steve knew how the man got so fat, but he still did not know where he could buy such big overalls.

Markie and Steve could hardly get all their food down because the portions were designed for big men and not little boys, even though those boys were big eaters. Uncle Jerry's eyes twinkled at them. "And now do you want some pie and ice cream?" he asked.

Markie shook his head and pointed to the fat man. "No," he whispered loudly. "I get fat like that! Then steer get me."

Uncle Jerry grinned even while he motioned for Markie to be quiet. "All right then. Let's go to the auction. Maybe they are ready to sell my steers by now."

They went in and found seats. The seats went up like stairsteps so everyone could see the pen at the bottom that held the animals to be sold. There was a door on one side of the pen to let a group of animals in to be sold and a door on the other side to let them out. A man with a whip guided them through. The auction-eer and a lady clerk sat up behind a desk where everyone could see them. Steve thought Markie's speech was much easier to under-stand than the auctioneer, who talked in such a steady stream that all his words ran together. But the buyers seemed to know what he was saying.

There were still some calves to be sold, and the boys were fascinated with the frightened little animals who skidded into the pen, danced around, and then scurried out the other door. Then several batches of pigs were sold. Markie's eyes got worried when at last the cat-tle began to be sold, but Uncle Jerry assured him that the big animals could not get out of the strong pen. Uncle Jerry's steers were some of the first cattle to come through, and after watching a few more lots, Uncle Jerry looked at the clock up the wall and said, "Well, boys, have you seen enough animals for one day? I think we had better be heading along home."

They left the sale barn and were soon on the road. They talked about the animals, sang awhile, and then Markie's head began to nod. Steve was glad that he had let Markie sit in the middle on the way, for now he was in the middle where he could visit with Uncle Jerry while Markie slept.

"Do you think Markie enjoyed the day?" he asked. Somehow after he had accepted the fact that Markie was along, he really had wanted him to have a nice time.

"Yes, I do, thanks to you," Uncle Jerry said. "There for awhile when he was upset, I didn't really know what I was going to do. You were a big help and I appreciate your unselfishness."

"I was kinda mad at him for a bit," Steve admitted, "but then I thought he acted like my little brother does when he is scared, and I decided I would help him get over it, just like I would for my brother. It worked."

"I'm not surprised he was scared of the cat-walk," Uncle Jerry said. "Down syndrome people are often scared of heights, and I wouldn't have wanted to force him. I guess seeing the fat man get squeezed by the steer is what made him fear the animals, but I think he got over it enough to have enjoyed the day. I had to think of that verse in 1 Thessalonians, Chapter 5, where it says, "Comfort the feebleminded, support the weak, be patient toward all men.' When we are with Markie, it is good to remember that, and I think you did very well today."

Steve felt warmed with Uncle Jerry's praise, but there was still one thing he wanted to know. "Uncle Jerry, do you think that someday I am going to be as fat as that man we saw at the sale barn?"

Uncle Jerry grinned down at Steve. "Not unless you do it on purpose. Did you admire him? Frankly, Steve, when I was your age, I was in the same shape you are, but good hard work, a growth spurt in my teens, and staying away from the cookie jar, put me in the shape I am now. I wouldn't worry too much about my weight if I were you. Eat all the potatoes, meat, asparagus, broccoli, cauliflower, green beans, and—"

Steve sighed a deep sigh.

"And go easy on the cookies, cake, pie, and candy," Uncle Jerry added. "And welcome hard work instead of running away from it."

"You told me that before," Steve said, "and I have been trying. But work is no fun!"

"It will be someday," Uncle Jerry said. "And if it isn't, you just do it anyway."

They were nearing home and Steve sat in drowsy contentment, while Uncle Jerry hummed to keep himself awake.

When they pulled into the lane, Jeff was

standing by the barn door. His jaw dropped in surprise when he saw Markie open the truck door to let Steve out. After they were gone, he turned to Steve and demanded, "Did you have any fun?"

"Sure did!"

"With Markie along?"

"Oh, we both had a lot of fun."

Jeff's face mirrored disbelief. "You've got to be kidding," he muttered, and Steve felt a moment's sadness for his brother. He knew Jeff had a terrible time appreciating Markie.

But it *had* been a wonderful day! Steve raced for the house as fast as his short legs would carry him. He could hardly wait to tell his whole family all about it.

4

Sue Hammond—
A Friend at Last

That Saturday morning Sue Hammond was excited, as excited as any girl usually is when she hears that a new girl is moving into the community. Sue was especially happy because she had no girl cousins just her age, and neither were there any girls just her age at church or school. Sharon Kemp's mother had said that Sharon had turned thirteen in March, and that was just two months after Sue's January birthday.

Sue stirred the orange Jell-O dreamily. Mother was grating carrots to add to it for the salad they would be serving the next day when the Kemps came for Sunday dinner. The Kemp parents had been in the community several times as they made arrangements to move, but this was the first time they planned to bring their children.

"Mother, what do you think Sharon will be like?" Sue asked.

Mother stopped grating a carrot for a moment and smiled at Sue. "I don't really know because I haven't seen her, but her parents seem to be nice people. You are not worried she won't be nice, are you?"

"Oh, no," Sue said. "I'm sure she will be nice. I'm just hoping she will be like me. Do you think she will be pretty?"

"Does that really matter?" Mother asked. "What do you think she will be like? I can see that you have been imagining things."

"Oh, I just think that Sharon is such a pretty name that surely Sharon will match it. I think she will be tall and slender and graceful, with a sweet smile. I haven't decided yet whether she has blonde or dark hair, because her father is dark and her mother is light. I think she will like to sing—or maybe she will like poetry."

Mother brought the grated carrots over and added them to the Jell-O. Her eyes twinkled as she said, "Now it's my turn to do some imagining. I think Sharon will be on the short side,

56

with a slight weight problem. I think she will have protruding front teeth without the blessings of braces to correct them. I think she will have plain brown hair that doesn't stay in place—"

"Oh, Mother," Sue interrupted with a wail, "how can you talk like that!"

"Will it make any difference to you if I am right and you are wrong?" Mother asked. "Will you love Sharon less if she is overweight and slow and messy? I am expecting you to be kind to her no matter how she appears. I'm afraid you think too much about the appearances of people and not enough about their character."

"That's about what Uncle Jerry told me once," Sue admitted. "I really don't want Sharon to be perfect, or maybe she won't like me."

"She won't be perfect; I can assure you of that," Mother said. "I just hope she is a girl with a tender conscience and of good character, and I suppose her mother is hoping the same about you. See that you don't disappoint them. Please go downstairs and bring up those potatoes you dug this morning. We will need a good many because I called Aunt Bess, and she thought they would be able to come too. You know how delicious fresh potatoes are, and with those families—"

Sue was staring at Mother in dismay, and now she interrupted. "You invited Uncle Lorens too?"

"Why, yes. Bess knew Judith Kemp from when they taught Bible school together before they were married. They haven't seen each other since. Now if all plans carry they will be attending the same church. Isn't it amazing the way the Lord works things out sometimes?"

Sue fled down the stairs to the coolness of the basement. Resentment raised within her to a degree that she knew Mother would have little patience with. She wanted Sharon to like her. She was sure that first impressions were very important. What would Sharon immediately think of a girl who had a cousin who looked and acted like Markie? Often Markie tagged after her when he came to visit, and Sue did not really mind if there was no one better to associate with. She enjoyed reading children's stories to him and seeing his eyes glow. She liked to hear him sing. It gave her a good feeling to see the adoration in his eyes, and she did not mind too much if he gave her hugs. But she did not want Sharon to see him do these things. Sharon would surely find out about Markie sometime, but did it *have* to be the very first time she and Sue were together? Sue sighed and went slowly back upstairs carrying a large pail of potatoes.

Mother looked keenly at Sue's despondent face. "If Sharon judges you as less worthy for a friend simply because you have a cousin who is mentally handicapped, then I'm afraid she has some growing up to do. And it is unfair for you to accuse her of having such poor judgment before you even know her."

Sue scrubbed the potatoes thoughtfully. What could she say? Nothing could incite sympathy from Mother, she was quite sure. She hoped things would work out fine, but the excitement she had felt in the prospect of having a girl friend dwindled sharply. Probably Sharon would think she was queer and not even want her for a friend.

The next morning, however, dawned clear and bright, and the family hurried to get ready for church. As Sue helped her mother and older sisters straighten up the house and put the finishing touches on dinner, some of the old excitement returned. At last, before the day was over, she would have a real friend just her age, one with whom she could discuss things, heart to heart.

When Sue entered the auditorium, she immediately spied Sharon Kemp, who was sitting beside her mother. She could not observe her very well there, but in Sunday school Sue gave Sharon a big smile and introduced herself. She saw that Mother was partly right. Sharon was not really pretty, but neither was she homely. Her light brown hair was combed neatly back from a face that was lightly freckled across the nose. She wore glasses that partly shaded her mild blue eyes. She was several inches shorter than Sue, but she was not overweight.

Sharon smiled in return, showing slightly crooked teeth that in a way detracted from her looks. With a start, Sue realized from the uncertain air about her, that Sharon was just as apprehensive about this meeting as she was herself. Sue determined to help make Sharon as comfortable as possible.

Arriving home from church, Sue helped welcome the Kemp family into their home. Besides Sharon, the family consisted of David, the father, and Judith, the mother, plus James (who was a year older than Sharon), and three younger brothers. Because Uncle Lorens came also, there were too many people to sit at the table, so Sue offered to sit at the kitchen table with Sharon and refill water glasses and serving dishes, things Mother or her older sisters usually did. It would also give her an opportunity to get to know Sharon a little sooner.

Sharon was not a talkative person, but she answered all of Sue's questions about the school and the community she came from, her hobbies, and her family. Then Sharon asked Sue about her family. "And is Markie your cousin?" she asked.

Sue nodded reluctantly. Markie was being remarkably well-behaved at dinner, not chattering or banging his spoon or letting jelly dribble down his chin, but anyone could tell by looking at him that he was mentally handicapped. Sue hoped to avoid discussing Markie on this very first visit.

"He's a mongoloid, isn't he?" Sharon asked.

"Yes," Sue said. "Only Aunt Bess prefers that we say he is a Down syndrome child."

"I know," Sharon said. "But few people seem to know that term. 'Mongoloid' is rather like a nickname, and most people use it in referring to that kind of handicapped person."

Sue did not really want to discuss Markie, so she changed the subject.

A little later they were talking of the local Christian school and of how many were in each grade. "Will Markie be in our school, or does he go to a special school for children like him?" Sharon asked.

"He has always gone to a special school," Sue answered, "but Uncle Lorens wish they could find a teacher to assist at our school who has been trained to help handicapped children like him. Then he could be with us."

"That would be nice," Sharon said. "I think I would like that responsibility when I am grown up."

Sue was so surprised that she held her bite of blueberry pie too long in front of her mouth, and it plopped down onto her dress. Embarrassed, she jumped up and began scrubbing at her dress. Fortunately her dress was blue, so the slight stain did not show very much. Cleaning her dress gave Sue time to think. She decided that Sharon was a very unusual girl to even think of teaching mentally handicapped children. At least now she would not have to feel quite so uneasy about Markie if Sharon had an interest in him.

After dinner the women and girls gathered up the dishes and put the food away; the men went into the living room to visit, and the little children ran outside to play.

Sue's older sister offered to wash and dry the dishes, so the mothers accepted, and Sue and Sharon were also excused. Sue decided that a walk back to the creek would be enjoyable, and Sharon readily agreed. They went outside. Markie was sitting on the front steps playing with the cat.

"Hi, Markie," Sharon said, sitting down beside him. "What kind of animal is that?"

"A kitty," Markie answered, beaming at her attention.

"Does it have a name?"

"Yup. Bootsie."

"Because of her white feet, I suppose." Sharon smiled. "What color is the rest of her?"

Markie pursed his lips and gazed at the black, orange, and white cat. At last he shook his head and said, "Some of this and some of that!"

The girls could not help laughing, and Markie laughed with them. Sharon chattered some more with Markie, and Sue began to get restless. If Sharon became too interested in

Markie, perhaps she would be suggesting that they take him along on the walk. Sue did not want him tagging along.

At last Sharon joined Sue, and they wandered out behind the old barn and down the path that led to the creek. Sharon was strangely quiet, and Sue could not help worrying that perhaps Markie was the cause of it, just as she had supposed he might be.

When they came to the creek, they took off their shoes and stockings and dangled their feet in the water. Dragonflies swooped on brilliant blue wings and caught insects that the girls could not even see. Occasionally a frog would leap off a rock and into the water with a splash. Flies droned in the sunny spots. It was peaceful and Sue began to be sleepy.

Then Sharon said something that made Sue sit up straight. "Markie reminds me of my little sister."

"Little sister," Sue said. "You don't have a little sister, do you?"

"No," Sharon said quietly. "Not alive. She died the day before Christmas a year ago."

"Oh," Sue said, and she could not think of anything more to say. She had never had any experience in offering words of sympathy, but

Sharon looked so sad that Sue reached over and squeezed her hand. That seemed to be what Sharon needed, for words began to tumble from her mouth like creek water over rocks.

"I had always wanted a sister," she said, "and then at long last after the three younger boys were born, Sarah came. We knew immediately that she was different, and the doctors said she was a Down syndrome child. She had heart problems and had to have surgery almost right away. We thought she was going to die, but she pulled through and started to grow. Sarah had respiratory problems too, and got pneumonia several times. She took a lot of care but we loved her. She was so lovable and sweet." Here Sharon's voice became choky, and she stopped talking. Sue did not know what to say, so she said nothing at all.

"The doctors told us not to expect Sarah to live to be very old," Sharon went on, "but we thought if we gave her plenty of love and attention that she would be all right. But Sarah was only five when she died. She got pneumonia again and nothing anyone did, did any good. It was the saddest time there ever could be. People said it was best that she died as she wasn't normal anyway, but I have a hard time accepting that. Sarah loved life and helped our whole family to love it too. Children like that are special even if they aren't pretty. We learned a lot from Sarah even if she couldn't learn very much from us."

Thoughts tumbled through Sue's mind, things she had heard grown-ups say, things she had observed, things she had only vaguely felt. "But Sharon," she said haltingly, "perhaps you had already learned the lessons God wanted Sarah to teach you. So He took her away so she wouldn't need to suffer anymore."

"I know," Sharon said, "but I miss her. She was the little sister I always wanted, and now she is gone."

In quiet meditation the girls swished their feet back and forth in the cool water. Then Sharon stirred and with a note of hope in her voice remarked, "But if you share Markie with us a little now and then, maybe we won't miss Sarah so much."

Sue sat speechless as she recalled her fears concerning Markie and how she had imagined Sharon would react to him. Now here Sharon was suggesting that Markie's presence would be an aid in lessening their own grief. How strange life was! And how mixed-up she had been! Instead of considering Markie a liability, she ought to be rejoicing that he was still alive.

Having shared her deepest burden, Sharon seemed to be released in spirit. The girls chattered of other things as they put on their shoes and stockings and headed for the house. Neither of them expressed it, but there was an ease between them that had not been there before. Sue was certain she had found the friend she had always yearned for.

When Markie met them at the edge of the lawn, Sue thought to herself, *I was worried Markie might break our chain of friendship, and here he is the link to begin it.* He offered them each a bouquet of daisies he had picked along the fence and beamed when they thanked him warmly.

The Kemps left for the minister's home to rest and freshen up for the evening services, and Uncle Lorens went home. Sue took a blanket and a book out under the maple tree and tried to relax, but her thoughts remained on Sharon rather than her book.

At last she went into the house and popped a big bowl of popcorn and made some Kool-Aid. Filling a small bowl with popcorn, she carried it out to the porch and offered it to Mother who was sitting on a lawn chair writing a letter.

"Thank you, Sue." Mother smiled. "Did you have a good time today?"

Sue nodded. "Sharon's nice, even nicer than I had hoped."

"Even if she's not tall and graceful," Mother teased gently. "Does she like poetry?"

Sue grinned. "I never even asked her."

"And it doesn't make a bit of difference, does it?"

"Not really. You were right, Mother. I will love her for herself, and not for what I thought she might be." Sue suddenly sobered. "Mother, do you think Markie will live much longer?"

Mother had also learned of the Kemps' sorrow during the afternoon's visit, so she understood without being told why Sue asked the question.

"We have no reason to be especially concerned about his health right now," she answered. "He does have a tendency to get bad colds, but other than that, he doesn't have some of the health problems that many Down's children have. Lorens have always been thankful for that."

Sue felt strangely relieved. After hearing Sharon's sad story, even the thought of losing

Markie hurt.

She sat on the steps and munched popcorn, trying to sort through the things she had learned that day. When she felt she could say it right, she said, "Mother?"

Mother looked up. "Yes, Sue?"

"You know, I always thought of Markie as a shame and a waste. A waste because of the person he might have been if he were not a Down's child. But he's not, Mother. He's a gift, a gift to his family so we can be better people than we would be if he were not a Down's child."

Mother smiled. "You have learned something valuable, my child, and you have expressed it very poetically. All the babies to whom God has given life have a purpose to fulfill here on earth. We dare not have careless, unloving attitudes toward them even if they are not pretty or intelligent or healthy. Markie *is* a gift and we should accept that gift gratefully. We should also be charitable of ourselves, Sue, if we have physical imperfection. Of much greater importance is our character."

"Sharon seems to have a good character," Sue said thoughtfully. "And even if Markie is mentally handicapped, he does have good character. I've learned a lot from him. He is obedient, accepting of others, and forgiving. I hope he lives a long, long time!"

Mother and Sue sat in comfortable silence until a stirring within the house told them they had better join the others in getting ready for church.

5

Marilyn Hammond— A Vivid Imagination

Marilyn Hammond felt very frustrated. The evening had started out happily enough with all the Hammonds coming to Grandpa Hammonds to celebrate Grandma's birthday. Grandma's children had brought chicken to barbecue and all the good things that go with it, telling her that she was to relax and let them do the work. She bustled here and there, however, ordering them what to do just as she had always done, while the grandchildren looked on with amusement to see their dads and moms being bossed around.

Getting ready for supper had been fun, and eating it had been fun. And after things were cleared away, the women sat chattering about their gardens and children, and the men discussed their jobs, the church, and world affairs. The children had scampered here and there and eventually organized a game of kick-the-can. It was fun playing in the dusky darkness when venturing too far from the yard light or the glow from the windows sent tingles of fear racing along the spine, and it was easy to jump at every little sound. Even the teenagers were playing, and that made it even more enjoyable for the younger children.

But now the fun was all gone for Marilyn. The problem was Markie. Markie often played with the younger children, but tonight he insisted on tagging after the middle cousins. They seemed to think it was her responsibility to see that Markie had a nice time. He was willing enough to cooperate in the game, but his short legs and slow reflexes meant that he and Marilyn were always the first ones to get caught. When someone came in and kicked the can, freeing them, their names were often called by the one who was *it* before they ever got out of sight. It was frustrating to say the least. Marilyn was quick on her feet and although she was the smallest one playing, she was sure she could outrun and outwit some of the older children who fell over their long legs or stumbled into each other. Quite often she could slip between them and make it to base. That is, when she did not have Markie tagging along.

Barry had been kind enough to take him on a round or two, and Sue had said she would like to, but it was difficult running with Markie when she was so tall and he was so short. Steve had enough problems maneuvering his stout little body around the yard without being hampered by Markie. And Jeff never seemed to notice Marilyn or Markie at all. He seemed determined to keep up with the older boys and did not have time to notice the smaller ones.

"Quit jumping around so much," Marilyn told Markie rather shortly. "Watch now. I think I see one of the big boys over by that tree. If he comes in and kicks the can we have to run. Fast! No poking around. Do you hear?"

"Ya. Run!" said Markie, still jumping up and down in excitement.

The girl who was *it* ventured too far from the can and suddenly a tall form swooped in, gave the can a mighty kick, and those who had been caught previously scattered into the shadows. Only a few names were called, and they were not Marilyn's or Markie's. Marilyn sighed with relief. She stealthily guided Markie through the gloom until she touched the wooden fence that bordered the yard and the neighbor's pasture. They sat in peace and safety behind the lilac bush, Markie's labored breathing the only thing that might give them away.

Marilyn was still irked with having Markie as a shadow by her side, his sweaty, sticky hand clutching her wrist. How much she would like to race in and kick the can and set all the captured ones free!

Suddenly a thought struck her. She knew the thought was neither kind nor honorable, but right then she did not care.

"Markie," she whispered. "Do you think this is a strong fence?"

"Strong fence?" he repeated, sounding puzzled.

"I sure hope it is," she said. "Because I know the neighbor has cows in that field. I saw a whole herd of them right along this fence before supper. Cattle can see in the dark, and they can smell really well too. I guess they can see or smell us right now. I hope they don't mind us being along this fence like this."

"Let's go!" Markie stammered, struggling to

his feet.

Marilyn pulled him back behind the lilac bush. "Don't! You want to get caught? I see the one who is *it* walking around under the light. She'll see us for sure. The cows can't get us anyway as long as we are on this side of the fence. See, this is a strong fence." She reached out and gave the wooden rail a hard push. It screeched alarmingly, and Markie grabbed Marilyn and whimpered. The girl who was *it* came closer and peered through the darkness, trying to see who was lurking in the shadows. Someone raced in and kicked the can, and for a moment the yard vibrated with shouts, running feet, and cries of dismay. Markie whimpered again, but Marilyn clamped her hand over his mouth.

"Sh-h, we'll get caught," she said. "We'll stay here for a little bit longer."

"Go in!" Markie said. "Cows get us."

"They can't get us," Marilyn said, delighted that her scheme was working so well. "Besides it's not the cows I'm worried about. It's the bull. That's the daddy cow. He's big and strong and sometimes he'll get mad and paw in the dirt. I think maybe *he* could knock this fence down."

Marilyn could feel the terror course through

Markie as he grabbed her even tighter. "Go—go in!" he begged.

"Well, go in then," Marilyn said, feeling terribly guilty and yet relieved at the same time. If Markie got scared badly enough, maybe she would never again be bothered with him when the cousins played games together.

"No, no," Markie blubbered. "Come with me. Cows get me. Daddy cow get me!"

"All right then," Marilyn said. "Come on."

She led Markie around the lilac bush and came face to face with the girl who was *it*, who promptly ran off to touch the can and call their names. But Marilyn explained to her that Markie wanted to go in. She nodded and Marilyn led the sniffling Markie into the house. But suddenly she did not want to go in with him. She did not want to face Mother or the other questioning aunts when they tried to calm the sobbing Markie. She slipped out onto the porch and sat on the swing. She should have felt as free as a bird now that Markie was gone, but she did not. She felt tired and depressed. She rocked to and fro listening to the merry shouts of the other cousins, but glad for the darkness and emptiness of her own little corner.

Just then the house door opened and a man peered out. He saw Marilyn sitting in the swing. Uncle Jerry looked down at Marilyn.

"Not playing with the other children?" he asked.

"Not right now."

"You didn't get into a fuss about something, did you?"

"No, I just got tired of playing."

"I suppose that's a lot of running for your little legs," Uncle Jerry said sympathetically. "Did you ever get a chance to kick the can?"

"Not when I had Markie with me. He's so slow."

"But it's nice of you to help him play," Uncle Jerry said. "You enjoy that, don't you?"

Marilyn wished Uncle Jerry would go back into the house. One part of her wanted to confess her unkindness toward Markie, and the other part of her was determined not to. She knew Uncle Jerry would be disappointed in her, and she did not like to disappoint him. His sad eyes always got sadder, and Marilyn did not like to see people sad. Really, the thought of Markie's sadness dismayed her more and more as she pondered it. Dismally she pushed the swing back and forth and did not answer Uncle

79

Jerry's question.

Uncle Jerry looked at her keenly and then said, "Well, I'm going to go out and call the children in. The older ones, that is. But you come in, too. I think it is best that you hear what I have to say."

Much puzzled, Marilyn gathered with the older children, the aunts and uncles, and Grandpa and Grandma in the living room. The little children were downstairs playing in the playroom. Uncle Jerry seemed to be the master of ceremonies. When everyone was seated, the grown-ups on chairs and the young people on the carpet, Uncle Jerry stood in front of the fireplace. There was no fire, because it was too warm, but lamplight shone on Uncle Jerry's face and illuminated the scar that jagged down the side of his face. Marilyn thought it was a shame his handsome face should be disfigured so badly.

"It is a pleasure to be with you all," Uncle Jerry began formally. "It is a pleasure to be able to gather in honor of our dear mother, whom the Lord has blessed with many years. We hope He sees fit to give her many more. But that is not what I want to talk about at the close of this gathering. The things I am about to say, I would much rather never disclose to anyone, although many of you know the story well. However, I have heard snatches of resentment and discontent from some of you young people toward your parents and the church."

Here Uncle Jerry looked down at several young people gathered near him, and they promptly looked away. Uncle Jerry loosened up as he went on. "I want to tell you the story of my younger days in hopes that you will understand how important it is never to take the downward steps of sin and rebellion."

Uncle Jerry ran his finger down the scar on his face. "Did you ever wonder how I got this scar?" he asked. "Oh, I know your parents told you I got it in a motorcycle accident, and that is true, but there is so much more to it than that."

Marilyn sat very quietly. She had always wondered how Uncle Jerry got the scar, but as he unfolded the story of his younger days, she sat in bewilderment and pain. Sue sensed her distress and seemed to understand, for she reached over and took Marilyn's hand. In a voice sometimes thin and trembling, sometimes plain and bold, Uncle Jerry told of his rebellion against his parents, his use of alcohol, tobacco, and drugs, and his marriage to a woman who did not love him, the birth of his son, Ricky, and finally the motorcycle accident that brought him to the brink of death, and the long road home. Marilyn could not understand it all, but she understood the horror of sin, and that it had all happened to her dear Uncle Jerry. He spoke sternly to the young people of the awfulness of rebellion and of the terrible reaping, but he also spoke of the love of Jesus and His forgiveness. Uncle Jerry had been forgiven, but he had a small son and a wife a thousand miles away who would have nothing to do with him.

The thought of having another little cousin whom she had never seen and perhaps never would, was almost more than Marilyn could comprehend. She mourned with Uncle Jerry as his voice broke, and he wiped his eyes when he talked of little Ricky who would grow up never knowing his own father's love. Because of the accident that threatened Uncle Jerry's sanity and ability to support a child, the mother had gotten custody of Ricky and had taken him far away.

"The reaping of sin is terrible but just," Uncle Jerry said. "I thank God for His forgiveness and healing, but I want you all to pray with me that someday Ricky and his mother will come to know the Lord."

To herself Marilyn promised to pray for Uncle Jerry and the family he could not claim. No wonder sadness seemed so often to rest on his face. No wonder he had no interest in other women. No wonder his nieces and nephews were so dear to him, filling somewhat the void in his life. Marilyn promised herself that she would be extra kind to this uncle whose own little boy was so far away.

She suddenly noticed Markie sitting on the floor with his head in Aunt Bess's lap. His tears were gone, and now he merely looked sleepy, but when he saw Marilyn gazing at him, he gave her a reproachful look. She felt guilty as she thought of the fear she had planted within him, a fear based on her untrue story.

Uncle Jerry sat down and gradually the group in the living room broke up, the young people looking more sober than Marilyn had ever remembered them looking. Marilyn edged over to Markie. "Here Markie," she said, handing him a piece of candy Grandma had given her earlier in the evening. "You may have it. And Markie, there was nothing out by the fence that could hurt you. I don't know if there was a daddy cow in that field or not. I'm sorry I said that."

Aunt Bess gave Marilyn a knowing smile and squeezed her shoulder. "I know it takes patience, Marilyn," she said. "I'm sure you're forgiven. Thank you for playing with Markie as well as you have been."

While Mother was gathering up the little children and Dad was bringing the car up to the house, Marilyn went to find Uncle Jerry. She found him on the front porch sitting in the swing. His shoulders sagged and he looked worn out, as if the talk he had given had taken more from him than he could endure.

Sympathy and love filled Marilyn as she stood in front of him, with tears in her eyes. "Sit down, little one," he said, moving over. She sat beside him. Feeling strongly the need to clear herself of her unkind and untrue actions toward Markie earlier in the evening, she now told Uncle Jerry all about it.

"So you were exaggerating again?" Uncle Jerry said. "A vivid imagination is a handy thing at times, but not when you harm others and deceive them. I'm glad you cleared yourself with Markie. I figured something like that happened when he came in crying and fussing

84

about cows getting him. Do you really mind so much having to be his right-hand helper? I thought you were doing very well."

"It's just that I always get stranded with him, and then I get caught first when I wouldn't otherwise. Sometimes I am left behind or they won't let me play because then Markie will insist on playing too or something . . ."

Uncle Jerry nodded sympathetically. "Just be patient. I know the others are trying hard to accept him. Barry has come a long way. Steve and Sue are doing much better. If you are kind to a weaker person, it will make you stronger, and you will be rewarded either in this life or in the life to come. As for Markie, sometimes I wish Ricky had also been born with Down syndrome."

Marilyn turned eyes of astonishment to Uncle Jerry. "But why?" she asked.

"Because Markie will always be innocent before God. His soul will never be corrupted by the sins of this world. If my son were mentally handicapped I would not have to worry about his soul, and besides, probably his mother would not want him, and she would give him to me."

Marilyn nodded. She had learned so many

things this evening that her brain whirled trying to understand. "I never thought about that," she said. "I do wish you could have your own boy. I never knew I had another cousin, but now that I know, I wish I could see him. I'm sure he would love having you for a father if he only knew you. You are so kind, it is hard to believe you ever were bad."

"That is because of the love of God," Uncle Jerry said softly. "He can save the worst sinner."

"I guess we nieces and nephews will have to be your children for now," Marilyn said. "You are so kind to us that we all love you."

"You are a comforting child," Uncle Jerry said gently, "but listen. I hear your father calling. You had better go. Good night, Marilyn."

"Good night, Uncle Jerry."

6

Jeff Hammond—
Day of Disobedience

Jeff Hammond pushed the dark hair out of his eyes and sighed. It took so long to fill the big 4020 John Deere with diesel fuel, but Dad had ordered that the tractor be refueled. Dad was going to David Miller's, who lived a half mile down the road, to help with emptying his manure pit. Jeff hoped Dad would ask him to go along.

Just then Dad came out of the machine shed. "All ready, Son?" he asked. "I'm going to have to be getting along or the afternoon will be gone before I know it. It may be a little late till I get home this evening. At four o'clock you and Markie can go bring up the cows. Get them in and fed and get everything ready for milking."

Jeff stared at Dad. "I thought I could go with you!" he blurted. "And this is Steve's week to go after the cows."

"I need you here at home," Dad explained. "Mom is taking the girls over to the church to clean and then taking Steve on into town to the dentist. The little ones will go with the girls, but Markie may as well stay here with you."

"Why can't Markie go with Mom? I hate baby-sitting for a retard. He doesn't know how to do anything but get in my way." Jeff knew he was treading on dangerous ground, but he was too upset to care. It was bad enough staying home and doing the chores; having Markie around was the absolute limit!

"Mom's taking the little car or else Markie could ride along," Dad said, "and you are not to call Markie belittling names. He is a human being with feelings and a never-dying soul just like you. You would do well to remember that. Make sure you treat him kindly this afternoon when we're all gone. He adores you boys. See that you are worthy of his adoration."

"But he's such a nuisance," Jeff complained. "He tags after me, is always in my way, asks stupid questions, and just about drives me funny. I can't see why he has to be here so long anyway."

Dad's dark eyes, as expressive as Jeff's own, let it be known that he was upset. "Listen here, young man. There are a good many things you could learn from Markie if you were wise enough to admit it. For one thing, he knows how to obey without a lot of questioning and complaining. That is more that I can say for you lately."

Jeff knew what Dad said about him was true. He did have a hard time obeying. It seemed that so many of the things Dad requested were unreasonable. Markie was obedient. It took a great deal of patience on the part of Aunt Bess and Uncle Loren to teach Markie what he ought or ought not to do, but once he understood, he performed their commands very diligently. Jeff thought he obeyed because he was too slow to think of any alternatives.

Dad went on. "Learning comes easy for you, Jeff, and that can be a real blessing. You like to use big words and give your opinions on all sorts of subjects. But intelligence can also cause you to have a high opinion of yourself and look down on people like Markie. Do you know that unless you are submissive and obedient, you are not wise, no matter how much you know? I have the feeling that Markie could teach you a great deal if you would be patient enough to learn."

This time Jeff knew better than to say a word other than, "Yes, Dad."

He watched with Markie as Dad got into the big tractor with the honey wagon behind and roared down the road. They watched as Mom and the rest of the family got into the car and left for town. Jeff despised going to the dentist, but for once he thought that would be preferable to spending the afternoon at home alone with Markie.

Jeff knew his feelings about Markie were unjust because his cousin had done nothing to cause problems in the four days he had been with them. Markie's parents had returned to their former community to attend a wedding and to bring back some household items they had not brought with them previously. They thought it would be a good time for Markie to get to know these cousins a little better, considering that they lived in another community and he did not see them often. The rest of the family had welcomed Markie royally, and the little ones were delighted with their new playmate who always had time for them. Mom said that when the children sang together it "rivaled the birdies."

When all was quiet, Markie turned to Jeff and said, "Let's work!"

"Naw," Jeff muttered, kicking at a tuft of grass in the lane. "There's nothing to do yet. Guess I'll go in and read awhile."

Markie trailed behind. When Jeff got his book and sprawled out on the davenport in the living room, Markie went to the bookshelf and found himself a book too. Soon he was murmuring to himself as he slowly paged through the book, a favorite of the little ones. It irked Jeff and he glanced up, ready to tell Markie in no uncertain terms to be quiet, but he watched Markie and became fascinated as he observed the concentration on the face of the handicapped boy. Markie would look a long time at a picture and then painstakingly sound out each of the words on the page. It took him a long time but he persevered.

"I suppose that is what Dad meant when he said I could learn something from Markie," Jeff thought ruefully. "I'd never have the patience to read if I had to work so hard at it. It would be worse than algebra for me."

Markie finished the book and carefully put it back on the shelf. He selected another, and Jeff went back to reading his own. After some time, he heard Markie give a long sigh. He slid off the big chair and came bringing the book to Jeff. "Can't read it," he said mournfully. "Read me a story about Jesus."

Oh, no, Jeff groaned to himself. *This is the limit. Reading to an eleven-year-old!* He did not like reading aloud anyway, but he took the book, and Markie sat beside him, beaming happily. Jeff meant to read so poorly that Markie would soon become bored and run off, but somehow Jeff did not feel right about reading Bible stories disrespectfully, especially not when Markie listened so raptly, absorbing every word. The story of Jesus blessing the children had a picture on the page. Markie looked at it a long time. Then he looked up at Jeff and said, "I love Jesus. He is so good. So good! You love Him, Jeff?"

"Of course, I do," Jeff answered shortly. But the question bothered him. Maybe this is what Dad meant about him learning from Markie. Maybe he should have simple faith like Markie's, and the same uncomplicated love. He went back to reading his own book and Markie

94

wandered outside.

He became lost in his reading until Markie came and stood in the doorway. "Time to work?" he asked hopefully.

Jeff glanced at his watch and started guiltily. Four o'clock! And he had not even thought about chores. He bounded to his feet. "Righto," he said. "Let's go get the cows."

He was not happy about taking Markie along to get the cows. Markie was a slow walker. If they had started out earlier it would not have been a problem, but this way they would have to hustle right along. And then, of course, Dad persisted in putting the cows in the back pasture during the day. The pasture was the farthest point you could go on the farm, and Jeff thought it was ridiculous even to think of pasturing cows there. That was why Dad had bought the Morgan colt at the auction—to train for getting the cows easier and quicker.

The colt! Of course! Why had he not thought of that earlier? Markie could stay at home while he quickly went back and rounded up the cows. It would take only half the time. Dad had forbidden the boys to take the horse out alone, although they had often ridden him under Dad's tutorship. Star was nearly grown now and Dad had said they could soon use him around the farm, but he did not want the horse spoiled by boys who did not know what they were doing. But Jeff felt sure he knew what he was doing. He led Markie to the lot behind the barn where Star and a few sheep grazed.

"I'm going to catch Star and ride him out to get the cows. You stay up by the barn while I'm gone," Jeff told Markie, trying to sound persuasive.

Markie's eyes widened. "Star? Ride Star? Uncle Tim said, 'No! No!'"

"Ah, Dad won't care. Star's pretty well trained now. Dad's just too cautious. He's afraid I'll teach him some bad habits, but I won't. I wasn't born yesterday." Jeff held out the cat scoop to Star, and he readily came to the rail fence where Jeff slipped his halter on. Dad had trained Star to be ridden bareback, so Jeff did not have to bother with a saddle. He mounted the horse and looked down at Markie. Markie backed off and gazed at Jeff with a mixture of disapproval and fear in his eyes.

"Uncle Tim said, 'No, no!'" Markie said again.

"Well, so what," Jeff said. "Let the rails down, Markie, so I can come through now, and put them back up after I'm gone, so the sheep don't get out. That's a good boy."

"Uncle Tim said, 'No, no!'" Markie scolded again as he struggled to replace the rails, and Jeff was glad when Star's prancing feet drowned out the sound of his cousin's words.

"Stay by the barn now until I get back," he called to Markie and then guided the horse down the lane that would eventually lead to the cow pasture.

Jeff loved the feel of Star between his knees. The horse was sturdy and strong, and although he would never be a racer, he felt plenty fast when Jeff galloped him. Jeff did not plan to gallop him today, however. It would be better to be extra cautious, considering that Dad had not given him permission to ride. He and Star would get the cows and be back before anyone besides Markie was the wiser. He planned to bribe Markie with some candy he had stashed away in his drawer. Surely Markie could be kept quiet with candy.

The cattle lane, fenced in on both sides, wound through fields of corn and hay and soybeans. Jeff liked the way the cows wore paths through the grass. The dust was powdery where the cows walked, and it rose in little puffs as Star trotted along. After several fields, the lane entered a little woods. Jeff looked back and he could still see the barn and the little dot that was Markie standing beside it. Then he entered the cool shade of the woods. The soil was damp here and the cow trails had cut deeper. Jeff loved this part of fetching the cows, and if he had been walking he would have had a hard time resisting a sashay into the woods. Squirrels, chipmunks, deer, rabbits, birds of all kinds; you never could tell what you might see in the woods.

Suddenly, immediately in front of Star there was a mighty "Whirrr-r-r!" and a partridge shot out of a thick bush. Jeff was so startled he rose in his seat and pulled back on the rein. Star gave a frantic lunge sideways and Jeff felt himself lose contact with the horse. There was the instant of being airborne and the horrible thud of Jeff's body against a sturdy cedar fencepost.

He knew nothing at all after that until a persistent voice kept saying, "Jeff, wake up! Jeff, wake up! Jeff, wake up!"

Vaguely he knew it was Markie and half crossly he wanted to tell him to be quiet. He opened his mouth to talk, but his tongue felt thick and nothing came out. He opened his eyes and met Markie's. Tears were streaming from his cousin's eyes. Sweat stood out in huge beads on his forehead, and he was panting as if he had run a mile. For a moment disgust swept over Jeff. What was Markie having a fuss about now?

He moved and a searing pain bit into him, and he realized he was lying on the ground. A bramble scratched his cheek, so he attempted to sit up. His head felt enormous and almost too heavy to hold up, but he struggled to a sitting position and looked down at his body. His right leg was as long and lank as ever, but the left shot out at a queer angle. Jeff knew without further thought that it was broken. His right arm felt as if it were on fire. A glance showed him that barbed wire, with all its jagged cruelty, had run a furrow down his arm. Blood pumped with a steady stream into a pool forming on the ground. Seeing his lifeblood draining from him, already the nectar of flies, was too much for Jeff. He fainted.

When he awoke, he heard Markie puffing and saying, "There, that stop blood. Yucky blood!" With surprise he saw Markie's chubby tummy over him, bare and white. With clumsy fingers, Markie had wrapped his shirt around Jeff's lacerated arm. Jeff pulled it a little

99

tighter and was alarmed at how the pool of blood had increased during the time he had been unconscious. Fear coursed through him as he realized that if he did not get help soon, his life would be in danger.

"Markie," he said urgently. "Markie, get Dad." Somehow just then, Jeff wanted his dad more than he had ever wanted him before in his life.

"Where?" Markie asked. "Where's Uncle Tim?"

Jeff groaned. How could Markie understand? Could Markie understand anything? Would not even a dog be of more value than Markie at this moment? Jeff had read of a dog rescuing his master, but never of a retarded person rescuing anyone. But Markie was his only hope.

"Dad is at David Miller's unless he is home by now. Can you use the telephone?"

Markie shook his head emphatically, so Jeff went on to explain. "Well, then you will have to go down there and tell him what happened. Go out the lane and turn down the road on the side where the mailboxes are. Go past the white house and on to the farm with the three big silos. That's David Miller's. Tell Dad to come right away."

100

Markie stood looking down at Jeff as if he was undecided what to do. For a moment Jeff was afraid he still did not understand. Then Markie bent down awkwardly and kissed Jeff on the forehead. "I go now," he said firmly. "Jesus will be with you."

Feeling more humble than he had for a long time, Jeff struggled to find a more comfortable position in his misery. His head ached; he dared not move his leg even an inch or unbearable pain swept over him; and his arm throbbed. And now his conscience was also beginning to hurt. For some reason Dad's words from that morning kept coming back to him. "Do you know that unless you are submissive and obedient, you are not wise, no matter how much you know?"

"Well, I sure haven't been wise," Jeff murmured to himself. "If only I had obeyed." Tears of remorse and pain coursed down his cheeks. He wanted Dad to come quickly, but he was not at all certain Markie would be smart enough to bring him. Of course, Markie had known enough to come looking when Star had returned without a rider, but it was asking a great deal for him to go down a busy road and find Dad.

Jeff moved again to try to find a more comfortable position and somehow managed to get his broken leg into even worse shape. Pain swept over him and he fainted again. When he woke up, strong hands were lifting him onto a stretcher, skilled hands that knew what they were doing.

"Steady there, Son," Dad's voice said, and Jeff knew that everything would be all right. He drifted in and out of consciousness on the way to the hospital.

It was two days before Jeff really stayed awake long enough to be rational, and then he wanted his dad.

"Dad," he said, "I've been a fool. I thought I knew so much and deliberately disobeyed you. Even Markie knew better. He told me not to ride Star, but I did it anyway. I think a partridge scared him, but that's all I knew until I woke up to see Markie bending over me. Dad, I've been such a fool."

"That's what you said over and over when you were unconscious," Dad said. "And have you become wise, my son?"

"Yes, Dad," Jeff said quietly. "At least enough to know that I need Jesus in my life."

Jeff and Dad talked things over then until

everything was clear between father and son and between Jeff and God. Then Jeff fell into a peaceful sleep.

Later in the day when Jeff awoke, Uncle Jerry was there. "Feeling better, Jeff?" Uncle Jerry asked. "You had us worried there for awhile. You got help none too soon, but I suppose you realize that."

"I never asked anyone about how they found me," Jeff said. "Do you know?"

"You have a very brave cousin," Uncle Jerry answered. "I hope you realize that, Jeff. Markie followed your directions, I suppose, only he stopped at that first white house past your place, and insisted that the lady call the doctor. At first she thought he was crazy and feared that he had escaped from somewhere, but he kept saying, 'Jeff hurt. Jeff hurt. Leg broke. Blood, blood, blood!' She remembered there was a Jeff at your place so she called the police and the ambulance because no one answered at your house. Then she called down to David's. Your Dad and the ambulance got to your place about the same time. Markie directed them to you, and then he rather fell to pieces and needed medical attention himself, but he's all right now. In fact, he's wanting to see you. His turn is after mine."

"He took off his shirt and wrapped my arm," Jeff said, tears coming to his eyes as he remembered Markie's white tummy, bared for him.

"That is an ugly wound you have here," Uncle Jerry said. "They put in forty stitches. Barbed wire is awful stuff." Uncle Jerry ran his finger thoughtfully down the scar on his own face. "I hope you don't have a scar like this," he said softly, "but mine reminds me that I must obey God or reap the awful rewards of sin."

"I think mine will remind me not to be proud and disobedient," Jeff said.

"Then this whole experience will not have been in vain," said Uncle Jerry. "You are natured much like me, Jeff, and I feared for you, but if you have turned to the Lord early, you may not have to reap anything worse than a scar on your arm instead of many bitter memories. My time is up now, Jeff. God bless you and grant you healing."

Uncle Jerry left and Jeff looked expectantly toward the door. Now it was Markie's turn to visit. Could he ever thank him enough? Would Markie understand how sorry Jeff was for all the times he had scorned him? Jeff did not know quite how to tell him, but he meant to try.

7

Uncle Jerry—
The Family Gathering

Uncle Jerry mentally counted all the cars and decided to whom they belonged as he pulled his pickup into the crowded lane. Yes, the whole tribe was here, and he was the last as usual. Well, if he had not gone all the way to Cederton to Mary's Violetry he could have come sooner. But how could he forget the tradition he and his mother had begun so many years ago? On special days he gave Grandma Hammond a new violet for her collection, and she baked him chocolate chip cookies. Even in the years of his folly he had not forgotten, and when she could locate him, the cookies had always come.

"Hi, Uncle Jerry!" Steve greeted him from

the end of the walk where he was putting the finishing touches on a snow-shoveling job. "Look any better? Grandpa started it but I told him I could take over." He looked to Uncle Jerry for approval.

"Looks great!" Uncle Jerry smiled. "You're getting to be a real worker, Steve." He stomped the snow from his boots so he would not mess up Steve's careful job and went on up the walk.

He could feel the noise and bustle of the house even before he opened the door. This was the Saturday after Thanksgiving, traditionally the day when all the Hammonds gathered for a time of rejoicing and fellowship. To the children, it was a day for wintry fun if snow had fallen to purify the drab November countryside.

Grandma Hammond came to the kitchen. door. "Hello, Jerry. So you made it," she beamed, wiping her hands on her apron. Her twinkling dark eyes took in the large brown bag he was holding.

"I didn't forget, Mother," he said. "I hope it didn't get too cold. It's a Kingwood Red. Mary said it's a new kind."

"I'd love you even if you did forget," Grandma Hammond said. "And your cookies are in a blue pail in the freezer. Don't forget them." She took the violet out of the bag. "My, this is a lovely one. Such a deep burgundy." She showed the plant to several of the women and girls who gathered around to see Grandma's latest violet and then trailed her into the violet room.

The violet room used to be an east bedroom, but somehow the violets had just taken over as Grandma kept adding to her collection. At last they had removed the bed and Grandpa had built shelves and tables for the violets. Grow lamps gave the room a lavender glow. Violets of every shade and color grew luxuriantly because of Grandma's tender care. The women and girls loved the violet room, and even some of the men could not resist a stroll through it, especially in the wintertime when somehow the world seemed too empty of flowers. And Grandma never fussed if some of the wide-eyed, long-fingered little ones came in. "If they upset one," she would say, "usually there is at least one leaf unharmed so I can start another."

When the burgundy violet had found its own little place in which to grow, Grandma hurried out to the kitchen to help get dinner ready. It was a meal where everyone contributed something, so there was a great variety. The food was set out on the counter: a huge turkey, veni-son, vegetables, salads, pies, and other desserts. The grown-ups carried their loaded plates to the long table in the dining room, the little ones were seated at a table down in the playroom, and the older children and teenagers sat wherever they could find a place to sit down. The boys seemed to make it a point not to get too far from the food.

A feeling of sadness swept through Uncle Jerry as he watched the milling of the Hammonds as they tried to get their food in an orderly manner and failed entirely. Jeff and Steve's little brother spilled his water glass on the kitchen floor and then slipped and sat right in it. He howled. The aunts bustled here and there trying to keep things organized. Uncle Jerry could not help wishing his own little boy were standing in line and that he had a wife to mingle with the other women. He loved these gatherings, but he was lonely even in the midst of all the hubbub. But then, he told himself, perhaps it would be a long time before he could be at another Hammond gathering. He had better enjoy this one to the fullest.

When he had filled his plate, he sat down beside Markie who had decided to stay upstairs near his mother. "Lotta people," Markie said, waving his jelly bread in a sweeping motion. "Upstairs. Downstairs. All over."

"Right you are," Uncle Jerry chuckled. "Do you like it? Are you having fun?"

"Good bread," Markie agreed. "Good boys. Steve. Barry. Jeff. Poor Jeff. His leg's all broke. No fun for Jeff."

"Not much," Uncle Jerry said, glancing into the living room where Jeff had his leg propped up on a hassock, his crutches beside him. It was hard for active Jeff to be confined to the house for weeks on end. But Uncle Jerry was happy to see that the peace Jeff had found inside was being portrayed in his manner toward others and his circumstances.

When everyone had eaten all they wanted and the women were cleaning up the leftovers and doing the dishes, the young people and children began planning for their afternoon's activities.

"I've got the tractor and the wood wagon ready," one of the older boys announced, and then began the mad scramble as all the children tried to find their snowsuits, boots, mittens, and scarves. The older boys ran out and began a snowball fight, while the older girls helped the little ones into their wraps. Soon a colorful bunch of bundled-up children was milling about the kitchen and porch and trickling down the walk.

"Markie, are you going along?" Uncle Jerry asked, when he observed the boy standing in the kitchen with his mittens on and his coat over his arms.

"He thinks he wants to," Aunt Bess said. "But I've never let him go before. You know what bad colds he can get. I thought he should stay in with Jeff. Jeff can't go out because he can't keep his foot warm enough even if he would stay on the wagon. I think Markie should stay in."

Just then the kitchen door flung open and Barry and Steve burst in. "Aren't you ready yet, Markie?" they said. "Here, we'll help you get ready. Sit on that chair and we'll get your boots on. Where's your stocking cap?"

Aunt Bess opened her mouth to protest, but closed it again. Before she could make up her mind whether it would really hurt Markie to be out in the cold, they had him all dressed up to go out.

"I really do wish there were an adult along," she murmured. "I know the older ones watch out for the younger ones, but still it looks dangerous to me."

Uncle Jerry noticed the men in the living room had their Bibles out and were deep in discussion. He wondered what they were talking about. He hesitated and then said, "Well, get me a stocking cap and I'll go out with them. I suppose it will do my old bones good to be with the youngsters."

Grandpa Hammond had an old Ford tractor and a wagon that he used to bring in the winter's wood from the woodlot behind the house. The bottom of the wagon was filled with loose hay, and already it was full of little children and older girls. Behind the wagon the boys had attached two long ropes, one on each side. Every several feet they wrapped the rope around a tire. After three or four tires on each rope, they tied a toboggan. Several of the restless boys had already claimed a tire and some of the girls were on the toboggans. Uncle Jerry knew that before the afternoon was over, the children would change places a good many times as they fell off and someone else snatched their place.

"All aboard!" the driver called out. Uncle Jerry helped Markie up to a place beside him at the back of the wagon and checked to make sure there were no other dawdlers who would be heartbroken if left behind. He nodded to the driver, and the old Ford snorted as it began to pull its heavy load.

There was an immediate wail. The rope had come loose where it was attached to the wagon and one group was left sitting. Uncle Jerry tied the knot more securely than their young fingers could, and soon they were on their way.

They took a trail that wound through the woods and then came out on a little-used back country road. It was a beautiful day, just above freezing, with a bright blue sky. The last snow had fallen gently and the trees looked as if they had been dusted with powdered sugar. The fence posts marched by looking as if they wore bakers' caps on their heads. A few squirrels chattered from the oaks, wondering what possessed these noisy humans to swarm into their domain.

Uncle Jerry felt it was good just to be alive. Markie's cheeks were getting rosy. Marilyn flipped her auburn braids over her back and twinkled up at Uncle Jerry with eyes like stars. "Isn't this just the most fun! Let's you and me take the next toboggan ride. Okay?"

He had a fine ride on the toboggan with the courageous little girl hanging on for dear life. Then he bumped a long-legged teenage boy off a tire and rode there for awhile. He tucked a small boy on top of his crossed legs and the child thought he was on top of the world. He watched as Barry and Sue both raced for the same tire. When Barry reached it first, Uncle Jerry jerked the rope and Barry tumbled off to the side. Sue claimed the tire with a grateful grin for Uncle Jerry. He was happy to see that Sue was confident and cheerful and already losing much of the awkwardness that had plagued her for the last few years. She would never be beautiful in the worldly sense of the word, but she had a fresh-faced wholesomeness that he wished all girls possessed.

Barry hopped up on the wagon. "Markie, you want to ride on the toboggan?" he asked. "You can come back and ride with Steve and me."

Markie shook his head. "I fall off," he stated firmly.

"Ah, come on. We won't do any monkeyshines, and we'll hold you tightly. He can come with us, can't he, Uncle Jerry?"

Uncle Jerry motioned for the driver to stop, and he helped Markie to kneel securely on the toboggan. It gave him pleasure to see that the boys were truly concerned that Markie had a nice time. He wondered if they remembered how worried they had been that Markie would be nothing but trouble. What a difference a change of attitude made!

They were now going through the woodlot again. The trail was rough and ridgy. Uncle Jerry saw a look of desperation sweep over Markie's face. Suddenly they went over an extra big bump and Markie bounced off the toboggan. Steve rolled off with him. Uncle Jerry hollered for the driver to stop, but the boy was so intent on lacing the tractor and wagon through the trees that he did not respond right away. The children on the wagon raised up such a wail of dismay that at last it penetrated the noise of the tractor. The driver stopped promptly, sure by the look of distress on the girls' faces that something awful must have happened.

Barry looked back at the two chubby boys trotting up the trail and left his place to go and see that they were all right. Uncle Jerry could see that Markie was crying, but Steve looked cheerful enough. He saw Barry pull a big handkerchief from his pocket. Barry took the handkerchief and wiped Markie's eyes and held it to his streaming nose so Markie would not have to take off his mittens. Uncle Jerry felt a tightness in his throat as he saw Steve and Barry each take a hand of their handicapped cousin and encourage him on until he plopped exhausted onto the wagon. There, the girls and the little ones took over with their obvious concern, until by the time Markie got home, he began to feel like a hero. After all, he had fallen off just like the big boys!

At the house, most of the little ones, some of the girls, and Markie got off and swarmed into the house, anxious to get out of their cold, wet things and to tell of their adventures. Uncle Jerry pulled his stocking cap down farther, and though the house looked rather appealing, he stayed with the wagon. It really was better if an adult were along. The older boys sometimes forgot the fine line between good fun and dangerous play.

Finally everyone was tuckered out and the tractor and wagon were put away. The aunts had cocoa and cookies ready, and it seemed as if the children had forgotten that they had just eaten a big dinner a few hours before.

Uncle Jerry took his cup of cocoa and went

into the living room. There he found Jeff and Markie deep in a game of Candy Land. For the second time that day his throat tightened with emotion as he saw a cousin treating Markie with love and kindness. No way would proud Jeff have played such a baby game with anyone a few months before. God was certainly working in the lives of these nephews and nieces whom he had grown to love so much.

"Who's winning?" he asked.

Jeff looked up a bit sheepishly. "No one, yet," he said, "but I wouldn't be surprised if Markie does. Your turn, Markie."

"When you're finished with that game, let me know. Then I'm going to call in the older children and have a bit of talk."

Jeff's eyes darkened with remembered pain. "You're not going to have anything bad to tell us like the other time, are you? I mean about your former life and all that."

Uncle Jerry shook his head sadly. "No. That's not a subject I like to discuss. I wish I wouldn't have had to tell you about it ever. But perhaps because of those years, I have been brought to the decision I've made now."

The boys went back to their game and Uncle Jerry rounded up most of the older children.

They gathered around Markie and Jeff, who were just finishing their game, and cheered and counseled Markie until at last he won. "It was a good game, Markie," Jeff congratulated.

Then they turned expectantly to Uncle Jerry. There were not enough seats, so they sat on the floor with Uncle Jerry in the midst of them. "I could have your parents tell you, of course," he began, "but I think an awful lot of you all and I wanted to tell you myself. In two weeks I am going to be leaving for I don't know how long."

Blank dismay spread over the young faces before him, and Uncle Jerry knew in an instant that they loved him as much as he loved them.

"But why?" Sue wailed, for once completely forgetting her reluctance to speak before others.

"Where are you going?" one of the older girls asked.

"Well, first of all, I want to tell you the good news that I have legally regained visiting rights for Ricky. Before this, I was even denied the right to see him, but that is changed now. His mother has signed that I can visit him or have him visit me. Secondly, I have felt for some time that I ought to be doing something more with my life than just working at a job, raising a few beef cattle, and stashing away money. So I searched out places that needed volunteers of one sort or another. I thought of nursing homes, children's homes, rescue missions, and all kinds of places. I thought seriously of volunteering to work in a home for mentally handicapped children. However, it seems the Lord is calling me to work at a farm where young men who have gotten into trouble with the law are helped to gain new values of honest and hard work. I can put my natural abilities to work there, and I can also relate to the men because of my past life. I will have many opportunities to show them what Christ can do in the life of one who ran away from God."

"How far away is this place?" asked Barry.

"About 1,200 miles. I will be very busy there and will not be able to come home very often. It is much closer to where Ricky lives, and that is another reason I feel I should go there. I want you children to pray for me while I am gone that I can be used of God in this way. I will miss you all."

"I don't think we can get along without you," Marilyn said sadly, her green eyes aswim in tears. "We've learned so much from you."

"Like the fact that we are all handicapped in some way," Jeff said quietly. The middle cousins understood what he meant, and the older cousins sensed that it was not the time to ask.

"I'm glad if I have been a help to you. All you children have been a help to me," Uncle Jerry said. "Somehow when I was lonely or blue it seemed there was always a niece or a nephew to encourage me with a loving smile and a feeling that I was special. But we are all growing up in one way or another, and growing up means that sometimes we have to reach out and make new friends and do other work, sometimes very hard work. It is not easy for me to think of going away. Here at home you all love and accept me for how I am and how I look. I know that will not always be the case when I go out among other people. They may be suspicious of my scarred face or scorn me when they find out I am not living with my wife, although that is not my choice. But I have to grow up just as you do. But God will be with me and He will be with you. You also have parents who love you. They want nothing greater for you than that you grow up to become godly men and women. See that you never disappoint them as I did in my earlier years. God bless you all."

The older cousins drifted away to resume their game of round-table ping-pong down in the playroom. Only the middle cousins remained in the living room with Uncle Jerry and a few of the other uncles who came back to reclaim their easy chairs.

"Just look at Markie," Steve suddenly whispered. "He's sleeping like a rock!"

"Rather a noisy rock, I should think," Barry said, but there was no mocking in his voice. Markie had slumped over on the carpet and was snoring away, his mouth hanging open and his hair standing on end like the bristles of a brush. "Isn't it strange," Barry added, "that we thought Markie would be such a problem, and now we find that he isn't at all?"

Sue looked up from where she was arranging Grandma's afghan over Markie. "I guess the problem wasn't so much Markie, as us," she said thoughtfully.

"He didn't really change so much, but we did," Jeff said.

"I think from what Aunt Bess has said, that Markie has changed too," Uncle Jerry commented. "She says it is because even mentally handicapped children can sense when they are not wanted, and then they are apt to show off or become mean. You cousins and the church children have been kind to Markie, so he is kinder and sweeter than he was before. In turn, that makes it easier for you to keep loving him."

"The Golden Rule," Marilyn said. "It really does work if you follow the Golden Rule, doesn't it?"

"It certainly does," Uncle Jerry agreed. He felt more tired than he had for a long time. Muscles were beginning to protest from the energies of the afternoon, but it was a nice tiredness. He would treasure the memory of this little group before him: Jeff, with a new patience on his lean face; Steve, his round, merry face bringing cheer just by being himself; Barry, kinder and less of a show-off; Sue, blossoming into womanhood; Marilyn, a mixture of sugar and spice; and Markie, whose simple mind brought simple joys to those who learned to love him.

Just then the aunts came in and suggested to the drowsy uncles that perhaps it was time to go home. There still things to be done at home. Immediately there was a noisy rushing about as all of them tried to look for their wraps at the same time. Under cover of all the racket, Marilyn said to Uncle Jerry, "This has been ab-so-lute-ly the most glorious day, and I'm not 'zaggerating one bit!"

Uncle Jerry chuckled. "You are right, Marilyn, absolutely right. I'll remember this day for a long, long time."

THE END

Christian Light Publications, Inc., is a nonprofit, conservative Mennonite publishing company providing Christ-centered, Biblical literature including books, Gospel tracts, Sunday school materials, summer Bible school materials, and a full curriculum for Christian day schools and homeschools. Though produced primarily in English, some books, tracts, and school materials are also available in Spanish.

For more information about the ministry of CLP or its publications, or for spiritual help, please contact us at:

Christian Light Publications, Inc.
P. O. Box 1212
Harrisonburg, VA 22803-1212

Telephone—540-434-0768
Fax—540-433-8896
E-mail—info@clp.org
www.clp.org